MARK TEAGUE

ONE HALLOWEEN NIGHT

SCHOLASTIC INC.

New York Toronto London Auckland Sydney
Mexico City New Delhi Hong Kong Buenos Aires

For Lily

ISBN 0-439-75538-7

Copyright © 1999 by Mark Teague. All rights reserved. Published by Scholastic Inc.
SCHOLASTIC and associated logos are trademarks and/or registered trademarks of Scholastic Inc.

12 11 10 9 8 7 6 5 4 3 2   5 6 7 8 9 10/0
Printed in the U.S.A.   40   First Bookshelf edition, August 2005

The display type was hand lettered by Paul Colin. The text type was set in 14-point Martin Gothic Bold. The illustrations were painted in acrylics. Book design by David Saylor

n HALLOWEEN, Wendell, Floyd, and Mona were walking home from school when a black cat crossed their path.

"Don't pet it, Floyd!" cried Wendell. "Don't you know that black cats are bad luck?"

"That's just an old wives' tale," Mona said. "Besides, what could happen?"

Wendell merely shook his head. "Anything can happen on Halloween."

In fact, something did happen as soon as they got home. First, Wendell discovered that his mad scientist costume had turned pink in the wash. *This is definitely a bad sign,* he thought.

Then Floyd found out that he had to take his sister, Alice, trick-or-treating with him. "Pirates don't have little sisters," he complained.

Worst of all, Mona's mother insisted that she go out dressed as a fairy princess. "I look ridiculous," Mona protested.

"Nonsense," said her mother, and handed her a magic wand.

They all felt gloomy that evening as they set out trick-or-treating and hoped that no one they knew would see them.

But their troubles were far from over. At some houses,
they were surprised with tricks instead of treats.

At other houses, the treats were weird, or awful. Soon their bags were full of candy with names like "Broccoli Chews," "Sweet 'n' Sauerkraut," and "Eggplant Fizzlers."

"I can't believe this is happening," Wendell grumbled.

At that moment a screech of laughter came from down the block.
Floyd peered through his spyglass and groaned. "It's Leona Fleebish
and her nasty friends."

"Not them!" Mona squeaked. "They're the worst!"

"We'd better run for it!" cried Wendell.

Floyd led them down a hidden path through the woods behind the old Dreedle House. But soon Leona's jeering voice rang out: "We see you! You can't hide!"

The chase was on!

Finally, out of breath, they tried to slip behind some trash cans
at the end of a narrow alley. But Floyd ducked a moment too late,
and Alice's rabbit ears gave them away.
Leona squealed with delight.

Yo Ho Ho!
I see something funny.
It's Pirate Floyd
And his baby bunny!

The witches roared with laughter and slapped each other on
the back.

Floyd winced, but as he drew his saber, his face lit up with a pirate's grin. First, he kept the witches at bay so his friends could carry little Alice to safety. Then, growling like a movie pirate, he swung out of reach on an overhanging tree limb, turned a quick flip, and somersaulted backward over the fence.

"I didn't know you could do that," Mona said.

Floyd looked surprised. "Neither did I."

"Come on," shouted Wendell. "They're right behind us!"

They ran until they found themselves in an even stranger part of town.

"It's pretty creepy around here," muttered Floyd.

Wendell suggested they hide in the graveyard, but Mona scoffed. "You've got to be kidding."

"No, it's perfect. They'll never follow us into a place like this."

Actually, the witches didn't mind the graveyard at all.
"We see you, Wendell!" Leona crowed.

What's wrong with Wendell?
Let me think.
He must be MAD
'Cause he's dressed in pink!

The witches shrieked and hooted, laughing so hard
they nearly cried.

E.Z.
SMURKLE

1832
1871

EZ COME
EZ GO

R.I.P

FILBERT
SMOOT
1812
1877

BORN GRUMPY,
DIED IN A
BAD MOOD

MILDRED
FLINK
1808-1833

WAKE UP,
MILDRED!

For a moment Wendell's face turned as pink as his smock. But then an idea began to brew. He reached into his mad scientist's kit and started mixing potions. "Drink this!" he told his friends. "It will make us invisible."

At the word "invisible" the witches roared even louder. But their laughter turned to puzzled yelps when Wendell, Floyd, Mona, and Alice suddenly disappeared!

By the time the potion wore off, the children were several blocks away. Everywhere they turned, haunted houses creaked and moaned. "I've got a bad feeling about this," said Floyd.

"Can you make us invisible again?" asked Mona.

Wendell nodded. But when he opened his mad scientist's kit, it was empty, and suddenly the witches were approaching!

Before they could decide what to do, the witches were upon them. Leona cackled even louder.

Just look over there.
You'll see something scary.
It's Tinkerbell Mona
Dressed up like a fairy!

The witches squealed and guffawed. They snorted and wheezed and rolled on the ground.

Mona waited until the laughter died down. Then her eyes flashed, and suddenly so did her magic wand.

"Now I've got a poem for you," she said, and pointed her wand straight at them.

Ibbity bibbity, bobbity boad.
Leona fleebish, you're a toad!

Instantly, a bolt of white light shot out from the wand,
followed by a clap of thunder and a great puff of smoke!

The next thing they knew, Wendell, Floyd, Mona, and Alice landed right back on the corner where their evening had begun. There wasn't a witch in sight, and their bags were filled with wonderful, ordinary candy.

Wendell stared at Mona's wand. "How did you do that?"

She just shrugged. "You said anything can happen on Halloween."

Later, they sat in Floyd's living room, sorting their candy and sipping cocoa.

"You know, Floyd," said Wendell. "You make a pretty good pirate."

"Thanks. You're a good mad scientist too, even if you are pink. But Mona was the best of all."

She smiled. "I guess being a fairy princess was okay. Still, I'm sort of glad it's over. Now we can all get back to normal."

After a while, Leona Fleebish even stopped being a toad.